KU-022-457

Contents

THREE CHEERS,
SECRET SEVEN

ENID BLYTON

Hodder
Children's
Books

a division of Hodder Headline Limited

Copyright © Enid Blyton Ltd.
Enid Blyton's signature mark and the Secret Seven are Registered Trade
Marks of Enid Blyton Ltd.

First published in Great Britain in 1956
by Hodder and Stoughton

This edition 2002

The right of Enid Blyton to be identified as the Author of
the Work has been asserted by her in accordance with the
Copyright, Designs and Patents Act 1988.

For further information on Enid Blyton please contact
www.blyton.com

10 9 8 7 6 5 4 3

All rights reserved. No part of this publication may be
reproduced, stored in a retrieval system, or transmitted,
in any form or by any means, without the prior written
permission of the publisher, nor be otherwise circulated in
any form of binding or cover other than that in which it is
published and without a similar condition being imposed on
the subsequent purchaser.

All characters in this publication are fictitious and any
resemblance to real persons, living or dead, is purely
coincidental.

A Catalogue record for this book is available from the
British Library.

ISBN 0 340 79643 X

Typeset by Hewer Text Ltd, Edinburgh
Printed and bound in Great Britain
by Clays Ltd, St Ives plc

The paper and board used in this paperback by Hodder
Children's Books are natural recyclable products made from
wood grown in sustainable forests. The manufacturing processes
conform to the environmental regulations of the country of origin.

Hodder Children's Books
a division of Hodder Headline Limited
338 Euston Road
London NW1 3BH

[1]

No *meeting* after all!

'I don't see much sense in calling a Secret Seven meeting,' said Janet to Peter. 'There's really nothing to discuss – no adventure or mystery anywhere – and I did want to finish reading my book.'

'We haven't had a meeting for three weeks,' said Peter. 'And if you've got something better to do than to belong to the Secret Seven and attend the meetings, well, do it! We can easily get somebody instead of you.'

'Peter! Don't be so cross!' said Janet, quite horrified at the thought of not being a Secret Seven member. 'Of *course* I want to belong. But it's only *really* exciting when something is happening. Or if we've got plenty to eat and drink.'

'Well, if the others bring what they promised we should have quite a nice feast,' said Peter. 'Do help me to tidy the shed ready for the others, Janet – you just sit there and do nothing!'

The two of them and Scamper were down at the meeting-shed getting ready for the other five. On the door were the big letters, SS, and Scamper, the golden spaniel, sat outside as if guarding the shed. It was quite an ordinary shed in the usual way, but it seemed very important to Scamper when the Secret Seven held a meeting there.

'Here comes someone,' said Peter, as Scamper gave a small bark of welcome.

'Rat-tat!' There came a sharp knock on the closed door of the shed.

'Password!' called Peter. 'And don't yell it, please!'

'Lollipops!' said a voice, with a little giggle at the end.

'That's Pam,' said Janet. 'Come in, friend!'

Pam came in, carrying a small bag. 'Hallo!' she said. 'Am I the first? I've brought some biscuits – but there aren't many, I'm afraid.'

'Wuff-wuff!' said Scamper, from outside, and more footsteps could be heard.

'Lollipops!' said a low voice. And then another voice said, 'Peppermints!' and laughed.

Peter went to the door at once. George and Colin were there. 'Come in, George,' said Peter. 'Stay out, Colin; you didn't know the password.'

'Oh, come on! That was only a joke!' said Colin, hastily. 'Honestly it was, Lollipops is such a silly password – I just improved on it by saying "peppermints". Ask George if I didn't *really* know the password. I told him it coming along. Didn't I, George?'

'Yes – he does know the password really, Peter,' said George. 'Let him in.'

'Well, I will *this* time,' said Peter. 'Hallo, here comes Barbara – and Jack. But who's that waiting about over there?'

'It's *Susie*!' said Janet. 'That horrid sister of Jack's. I bet she'll try to come to the meeting.'

'Password, Barbara,' said Peter. Barbara and Jack both remembered it and went into the shed. Peter watched Susie for a few moments, but she didn't come any nearer, so he went in and shut the door of the shed. He left Scamper on guard outside.

'On guard!' he said, and Scamper sat down and waited, knowing perfectly well that he must bark if anyone came near. He watched Susie intently. If she dared to come one step nearer he would bark in his very fiercest voice!

Peter turned on Jack as soon as the shed-door closed. 'Whatever do you want to bring that awful sister of yours here for?' he demanded. 'You know how often she's upset our meetings, and got to know our passwords!'

'Well, she's promised not to come *near* our shed,' said Jack. 'And though I agree she's an awful nuisance, she does keep her word, you know. She won't disturb us, really she won't.'

'But why did you want to bring her at *all*?' said Peter. 'I don't trust her one bit. I bet she wants to play some silly trick on us.'

'She doesn't. But I'll tell you why I *had* to bring her,' said Jack. 'An American cousin of ours has sent her an aeroplane, and she can't fly it by herself. I'm longing to have a go at it. So we're going to fly it after the meeting somewhere. We've left it under your hedge till the meeting is over.'

'An aeroplane? What sort?' said George, eagerly.

'A *fantastic* one,' said Jack. 'As big as

this!' and he held his arms out wide. 'And it's got some kind of clockwork to wind up the elastic bands that help it to fly. I tell you, it's super!'

'Fancy sending an aeroplane to *Susie*!' said Peter, amazed. 'Why didn't your cousin send it to you, Jack?'

'Well, we were each asked what we wanted,' said Jack. 'I chose a cowboy outfit – it's fine – and Susie chose an aeroplane. Just like Susie to choose something *I* want when it comes. It's miles nicer than my cowboy-suit.'

'Would Susie let us come and see you fly it?' asked George.

Jack looked doubtful. 'I don't know. She's always rather cross about the Secret Seven, you know, because we keep her out of it.'

'I tell you what!' said Peter, quite changing his mind about Susie, now that she owned such a wonderful aeroplane. 'Let's *not* make this a Secret Seven meeting. Let's take our food into the garden somewhere, and tell Susie she can join us – if she'll let us help with the aeroplane.'

'Right,' said Jack. 'I'll ask her,' and out he went to speak to Susie.

He came back at once. 'Yes! She says she'll join our feast, and we'll go and fly the plane afterwards,' he said, putting his head in at the shed. 'Come on, bring out the food!'

So out they all went, and Susie joined them, grinning all over her freckled face.

'Hallo!' she said cheekily. 'We're not the Secret Seven this morning – we're the Exciting Eight!'

[2]

The beautiful aeroplane

Peter didn't like Susie's remark that they were not the Secret Seven at the moment, but the Exciting Eight. However, it wouldn't do to make her cross by snapping at her just when they all wanted a favour from her.

'Where's this super plane?' he asked.

'Where's this super food?' said Susie at once. 'We'll have that first before we fly the plane.'

'All right, all right. We meant to, anyhow,' said Peter. 'Where shall we have it? Over there under that tree?'

'No. I tell you what we'll do,' said Jack. 'Susie and I were going to fly the plane in the big field behind our house, so what about taking the food there and sitting on the grass? It's a nice field.'

'Yes. Good idea,' said Peter, and the others agreed. 'Come on, Scamper, walk-ie-walk!'

'Wuff!' said Scamper, pleased, and acted like his name, scampering off at top speed to the front gate. He stopped and gazed suspiciously at something hidden under the hedge, and then barked again.

'It's all right, Scamper, it's only my aeroplane,' said Susie, proudly. The Seven stopped to admire it. It stood there under the hedge, the biggest toy aeroplane they had ever seen, gleaming silver-bright in the sun.

All the children thought the same thing. Fancy that beautiful plane belonging to *Susie*. What a dreadful waste! But none of them said that, knowing perfectly well that if they did, the annoying Susie would pick up the plane and march off with it all by herself.

'Well, what do you think of it?' asked Susie. 'Better than a silly cowboy-suit, isn't it?'

Jack went red and glared at his sister. 'If I'd known that *this* was the kind of aeroplane our American cousin was going to send—' he began, angrily, but Peter stopped him.

'Don't go up in smoke, Jack,' he said, anxious to keep the peace. 'I bet your suit is super. But gosh, WHAT an aeroplane! It's even got retractable landing wheels, look!'

'Yes,' said Susie, proudly. 'In the leaflet about the plane, it says that the wheels go up into the body as soon as the plane starts flying, and are put out again automatically when it lands. I bet no one in the whole country has a model aeroplane that does that.'

The Secret Seven felt sure she was right.

Susie picked up the beautiful plane and went out of the front gate.

'*I'll* carry it for you,' said Peter. 'I'm sure it's too heavy for you!'

Susie laughed in her usual annoying way. 'What you *really* mean is that you're longing to carry it yourself so that everyone we meet will think it's *yours* and envy you!' she said. 'Ha, you're going red! *I* know you boys. But the plane is *mine* and *I'm* doing the carrying, thank you.'

Nobody said any more. What a pity Jack had such a clever sister. You could never get the better of Susie! She always had a smart answer ready. The little procession set out down the road, Susie first with the plane, then the others straggling behind and Scamper last of all, sniffing into all the corners as usual.

They came to Jack's house, went in at the side gate, and down to the bottom of the garden at the back. There they had to climb over a fence to get into the vast field that lay beyond.

'Food first,' said Susie, when they were all over, and Scamper had been lifted safely down to the ground.

'What food have *you* brought?' said Pam, who was beginning to feel annoyed with Susie.

'None. *I've* brought the aeroplane,' said Susie. 'I hope *you* haven't brought the miserable biscuits you bring to school to eat at break!'

'Shut up, Susie,' said Jack, uncomfortably. 'We've got a jolly good feast. You can have a very fair share, and remember that it doesn't cost you anything to be polite.'

The feast was certainly quite good. There were the biscuits, of course, some rock buns, pieces of gingerbread, an enormous bar of nut chocolate, jam-tarts, two bottles of lemonade, and a bag of toffees.

'Give Scamper a toffee,' said George. 'That will keep him quiet for ages.'

But Scamper wanted a bit of everything, and got it too. He had only to lie down by any of the Seven and look at them beseechingly out of his great brown eyes to get anything he wanted! Even Susie gave him a titbit and patted him.

'Now we'll fly the plane,' she said, when every crumb had been finished, and every drop of lemonade had been drunk. At once everyone stood up, excited. Jack took up the leaflet about the plane and studied it, while the other three boys tried to look over his shoulder.

'It seems easy enough,' said Jack.

'All I want is for you to show me what to do the *first* time and I'll know forever afterwards,' said Susie. 'Now, what happens?'

'Well, you turn this, that's to make sure the wheels go back as soon as the plane is in the air,' said Jack. 'And you press this, look,

Susie. And you wind up the key here – that's the mechanism that winds the elastic bands up tightly so that they give the plane the energy to fly, and—'

'I don't want all those explanations,' said Susie, impatiently. 'I just want to know how to *fly* the plane.'

Jack said no more, but pressed this and that, and wound the little key till it would wind no more. Then he held the beautiful plane high above his head and pressed a little button at the back.

'Fly!' he shouted, and threw the plane forward. It rose high into the air at once, with a loud, humming noise. It circled round beautifully while the children watched it in delight. Then it rose high into the air and flew off across the field to the other side, for all the world like a real plane.

'It will turn and circle back to us,' said Jack. 'That's what the booklet said.'

But it didn't! It kept straight on, flew over

a high wall at the other side of the field, and disappeared completely!

'Oh no!' said Jack, horrified, 'It hasn't come back. *Now* what are we to do?'

[3]

Where is the aeroplane?

'It's gone!' said Susie, looking quite heart-broken. 'My beautiful aeroplane! Oh, I wouldn't have let you fly it, Jack, if I'd thought you'd lose it on its very first flight. It will be smashed to pieces!'

'*I* didn't know it would do that!' said Jack. 'Whoever saw a model plane fly like that before? I never guessed it would be able to fly right across this big field. Oh, Susie, I'm awfully sorry, really I am.'

'Who lives in that place?' asked Peter, looking towards the high wall. 'Is there a house there?'

'Yes. It's called Bartlett Lodge, and it's a very big house,' said Jack. 'It's been shut up for ages, because the owners left to go abroad.'

'Oh, well, we could easily go and get the plane then,' said George. 'No one will shout at us or chase us if we look for it.'

'There's a gardener there,' said Jack, doubtfully. 'He's not very nice. When Susie and I lost our ball over there he wouldn't even let us climb over the wall to get it, though *he* couldn't find it. So we lost it.'

'*I'm* not going over,' said Barbara. 'I'd be scared. I don't like cross gardeners.'

'No one has to go if they don't want to,' said Peter firmly. 'Perhaps only four of us should go anyway. Eight is too many to make a quick getaway if necessary. We'll climb up to the top of the wall and see if the gardener's there. If he is, we'll be awfully polite, and apologetic, and ask if he's seen our plane. If he's *not* there, we'll go over and hunt.'

'Hadn't you better ask permission before you do that?' said Janet.

'Who from?' said Jack. 'There's nobody in the house to ask. Come on – we'll see what we can do.'

All the eight, and Scamper too, went across the field to the high wall. 'How are you going to climb that?' said Barbara. 'It's terribly high.'

'We'll shove each other up,' said Jack. 'I'll go first and have a look from the top of the wall to see if the gardener is anywhere about.'

George and Peter pushed him up, and at last he was on the top of the wall. He looked down into the overgrown shrubbery on the other side. Through a gap he could spy an unmown lawn, but there was no gardener to be seen. He put his hands to his mouth and shouted.

'Hey! Anybody there?' He listened, but there was no answer. Jack called again. 'Can I come over the wall and look for our aeroplane, please?'

Then a voice suddenly shouted back.

'Who's that? Where are you?'

'Here, on the top of the wall!' yelled Jack. He turned and looked down at the others. 'I can see the man. He's coming. Perhaps he's got the plane.'

A man came quickly through the gap in the trees. He was thick-set, and broad-shouldered, and had a ruddy, surly face, with screwed-up eyes. In his hand was a spade.

'Now then, what are you doing on that wall?' he said, threateningly. 'You get off. This here is private property and well you know it! Do you know what I do to children who come in here? I chase them with a spade!'

'We don't want to come in,' said Jack, rather alarmed. 'We just wanted to know if you've seen our aeroplane. It flew right over the—'

'No. I've not seen *any* aeroplane, or *any*

ball, or *any* kite, and what's more if I find one it can stay here,' said the surly man. 'You've got a big enough field back there to play in without throwing things over here. If I find a plane I shall put it on my bonfire.'

'Oh, *no*!' said Jack, in horror. 'It's a very valuable plane, a real beauty. Oh please, *do* let me come down and look for it, it belongs to my sister, and I—'

'If it belonged to the Queen of England I'd not let you come in here,' said the man. 'Understand? I've got my orders, see? I'm in charge of this place while it's empty, and I'm not having any boys coming in here to steal the fruit, or—'

'I'm not a thief!' said Jack, indignantly. 'I just wanted our plane. I'll tell my father, and *he'll* come and get it for me.'

'*That* he won't,' said the surly gardener. 'Now you clear off that wall this minute, or I'll tip you off!' He held up his spade as if he meant what he said. Jack didn't want to be shovelled off like a sack of potatoes, and leapt down very hastily into the field.

'What a beast!' said Peter, to poor Jack, as the boy sprawled heavily on the grass, for it was a high jump down from the wall.

'YOU SEND ME BACK MY AEROPLANE!' suddenly shouted Susie, stamping her foot on the grass, tears in her eyes at the thought of losing the aeroplane on its very first flight. But there was no answer at all from over the wall.

'Oh, Susie, I'm so sorry,' said Jack, getting up. 'Listen, I'll go and get the plane for you, really I will, as soon as that horrible man has gone off for his dinner. I expect he goes at about twelve o'clock.'

Everyone crowded round Susie, feeling really upset about the lovely plane. 'Didn't you even *see* it anywhere?' asked Susie, in a fierce voice, turning to Jack. He shook his head dolefully.

'Listen,' said Peter, taking command

again. 'Two of us will go and watch at the front gates of that house, and then, as soon as we see that horrible gardener going off for his midday dinner, we'll know it's safe to slip over the wall and hunt for the plane. We won't go in at the front gates in case anyone sees us and tells the gardener.'

'Good idea,' said Jack, cheering up. 'You and I will go, Peter. What's the time? Gosh, it's almost twelve now! Come on, let's sprint down that little lane to the road that the house faces on. Hurry up!'

Jack and Peter set off down a narrow little lane that led from the field to the road on which the big house faced. They turned to the left in the road and came to the big gate that led into the drive of Bartlett Lodge. There was a second gate farther on that also led into the drive.

'You watch that gate, I'll watch this one,' said Peter. 'But hide behind a tree or some-thing. You don't want that gardener to see you. He's already seen you up on the wall, and he may recognise you and chase you.'

'Don't worry, I won't let him spot me, and if he does, I bet I can run faster than he does!' said Jack, and set off towards the second gate.

There was a workmen's shed a little farther down the road, and he decided to hide behind that. So he posted himself there. Peter went across the road and hid behind a bush that most conveniently grew there. Now, would that tiresome man soon come out?

They had waited about ten minutes when they saw someone coming out of the gate nearest Peter. Jack signalled to Peter, and he nodded back. It was the gardener, no doubt about that. Jack recognised the burly figure at once, and drew back behind the shed.

The man set off down the road and turned the corner. Jack whistled to Peter, and the two ran to the little lane together, to go and tell the others that the gardener had gone.

They were in the field, playing with a ball, waiting impatiently for the boys to come back. Susie was still upset about her plane, and had been making quite a lot of rude remarks about the Secret Seven. They were getting rather tired of her!

'Here are the boys!' said Janet, as they appeared in the field. 'Any news, Peter?'

'Yes. That man's gone to his dinner, as we hoped,' said Peter. 'Now we can try and get Susie's plane. We'll go over the wall as before.'

'I'm coming too,' said Susie, unexpectedly.

'You are *not*,' said Jack at once.

'Well, it's my plane, isn't it?' said the irritating Susie. 'I've got every right to go and look for it. I'm coming too.'

'YOU ARE NOT!' said Peter, in the voice that all the rest of the Secret Seven knew

well, and didn't dream of disobeying. But
Susie wasn't going to take orders from
Peter.

'I shall do as I like,' she said, defiantly. 'I
shall climb the wall too.'

'Well, I don't know how,' said Peter,
'because I shall certainly forbid anyone to
give you a shove up.'

He and Jack were quickly hoisted up to
the top of the wall by George and Colin.
Susie stood by, looking sulky. She turned to
the two boys near her. 'Now give *me* a
shove,' she said.

'Nothing doing,' said Colin, cheerfully.
'Peter's our chief, as you jolly well know,
and he's given his orders. Don't be an idiot,
Susie.'

'I'll climb up by myself then,' said
Susie, and she very nearly did, using every
little hole and crevice for her feet and
fingers! The others watched her angrily
– but to their delight she could not reach

the top, and fell down when she was half-
way up.

'Have you hurt yourself?' asked Janet,
anxiously. But Susie refused to cry or to say
she was hurt. She made a rude face at Janet
and stood up, brushing her skirt with her
hand. She walked a little way away from the
others, and leaned against the wall, whistling as if she didn't care tuppence for any of
the Secret Seven.

The boys had now disappeared from the
top of the wall. There was a most conve-
nient tree that leaned towards the wall just
there, and one by one the boys gave the little
leap towards it that enabled them to catch
hold of a branch and then swing themselves
neatly to the ground.

They stood there, all looking cautiously
towards the house, through the gap in the
shrubbery. No one was to be seen, of
course, and as the house was not over-
looked by any other, they felt that they

could go safely forward and hunt for Susie's aeroplane.

'I hope it's not smashed to bits,' said Jack to Peter, as they made their way through the trees and bushes towards the great untidy lawn. 'If it is I'll never hear the last of it from Susie. She never forgets a thing like that!'

They began to hunt for the aeroplane. First they searched the beds round the lawn, but no plane was there, only masses of weeds that made the boys wonder what the gardener did for his wages! They hunted in the bushes, they looked up into the trees, wondering if the plane had caught in some high branch.

'This is maddening!' said Jack, at last. 'Not a *sign* of the plane! Do you suppose that gardener found it and hid it away?'

'I shouldn't be surprised!' said Peter. 'He's surly enough for anything!'

They were now fairly near the great house. It looked very forbidding, for all the curtains were drawn straight across the windows. And then Peter suddenly saw the aeroplane.

It had landed neatly on a little balcony on the second floor of the house, and there it was, balanced on the broad stone ledge.

'Look, there it is!' said Peter, pointing. 'And if we climb this tree that goes right up to the balcony we can easily get it. It's not smashed. It looks perfectly all right!'

'You go up, and I'll keep watch down here,' said Jack. 'I don't know why, but I suddenly feel nervous. I hope that gardener hasn't come back!'

[4]

Something rather strange

Peter began to climb the tree. It was quite easy and safe. Jack stood at the bottom, watching him, looking all round now and again in case that bad-tempered gardener came back!

It didn't take Peter long to get up as far as the second-floor balcony. He climbed over it, and examined the aeroplane. Was it broken in any way?

Most miraculously it seemed to be perfectly all right, nothing bent or broken at all. It had, in fact, made a perfect landing in a very difficult place! Peter called down to Jack.

'Hey! The plane's not damaged at all. Isn't that a bit of luck? I'm wondering what

is the best way to get it down. I can't very
well climb down the tree with it because I
need both my hands.'

'Got a piece of string?' called back Jack.
'If you have, you could tie one end to the tail
of the plane, and let it down carefully to
me.'

'Oh, yes, of course! Good idea!' said
Peter. He always carried string about with
him, of course, as did all the Secret Seven;
you never knew when it might come in
useful in any sudden adventure, and, in
the opinion of the Secret Seven, adventures
were nearly always sudden!

Peter took the string out of his pocket and
undid it. Yes, it would just about reach
down to Jack. He began to tie one end to
the tail of the plane, marvelling at the
beautiful workmanship in it as he did so.
No wonder Susie was proud of such a
model. But oh, what a *waste* for it to belong
to her!

He carefully let the plane down to Jack, who stood with his hands outstretched, waiting to receive it, most thankful that it wasn't damaged. Now perhaps Susie would hold her tongue!

'I've got it! Thanks awfully, Peter!' he called up. 'Come on down, and we'll take it back to Susie.'

Peter glanced round the balcony to make sure that he was leaving nothing behind. The curtains of the balcony room were drawn across, just as they were in all the rooms of the house – but they did not quite meet in the middle. And then just as Peter was turning away to climb over to the tree, something caught his eye. Something red and glowing, shining between the cracks of the curtains just where they did not meet.

He stopped, astonished. Why, that looked like a light, or a fire burning in the balcony room! But it couldn't be – the house was shut up and empty!

Gosh, I hope a fire hasn't started up somehow, thought Peter, alarmed. I'd better peep through the window and see. Perhaps I can open the balcony window.

He went to the window and peered through the crack of the curtains. Yes, he was right, there *was* a fire glowing in the room! But wait a minute – it was a gas-fire, surely?

He pressed his face against the glass of the window, and, when his eyes became used to the dimness of the curtained room, he could see quite clearly that a gas-fire was burning brightly in the fireplace. What a very extraordinary thing!

He tried the window to see if he could open it, but it was fastened inside. Gosh, had the people left that fire on when they went away? What a terrible waste of gas! It certainly ought to be turned off.

He was just peering to see what else he

could spy between the curtains when he heard Jack's voice.

'Peter! What on earth are you doing? Do come down!'

'I'm just—' began Peter, when Jack called again, suddenly sounding scared.

'Peter! I can hear someone whistling. I think it's that gardener coming back. HURRY UP!'

Peter had a shock. Gosh, it would never do to get caught by that awful man! He shot over the balcony at once, and was climbing down the tree before Jack could call again!

'Come on,' said Jack, urgently. 'Whatever made you so long? I'm sure it's that gardener about somewhere!'

But there was no sign of the man, much to Peter's relief. It must have been someone else whistling. He and Jack tore down the garden to the bottom, and stopped to get their breath in the shrubbery by the wall.

'Listen, Jack,' panted Peter. 'I saw something rather odd in that balcony room. I think we'll call a meeting about it. So can you make Susie go off with her plane, and then we'll be able to plan a meeting this afternoon?'

'Oooh, what did you see? What's up?' said Jack, at once.

'No time to talk about it now,' said Peter, looking at his watch. 'Anyway, I'd rather tell it to everybody at a meeting. Come on, let's shin up this tree and get over the wall. I'll hold the plane and hand it to you when you're at the top.'

He called over the wall. 'Hey, are you there, Colin and George?'

'Yes! Have you found the plane?' called the two boys on the other side.

'Yes. We're coming over. Stand by to help,' said Peter.

He waited till Jack had climbed the tree and was sitting on the wall, and then handed him the precious plane, which Jack then handed down carefully to Colin. There was the sound of delighted voices at once!

Then up went Peter and was soon on the wall grinning down at the others. He saw Susie proudly holding her plane again, smiling all over her face.

'Better take it home straightaway, Susie,' said Jack, remembering that he had to get rid of his sister somehow.

'I'm jolly well *going* to,' said Susie. 'I'm not letting the Secret Seven fly it again!' And off she went, head in the air!

'Listen, Secret Seven,' said Peter, urgently. 'Meet this afternoon at half-past two. I've got something to tell you all. Not a word to Susie, though!'

'Right!' said everyone, excited, and Scamper barked too. Ah, was something going to happen at last?

[5]

A proper meeting

The Secret Seven met very punctually indeed that afternoon, for they were all very anxious to know why Peter had called such a sudden meeting. Jack arrived first, ten minutes early and quite out of breath.

'Lollipops!' he panted, and was let into the shed at once. 'I've given Susie the slip – I *hope*!' he said. 'She wanted me to go fishing in the ponds with her this afternoon, and I had an awful bother trying to put her off. I think she half suspects there's another meeting on. I ran like a hare as soon as I could give her the slip!'

'Bother Susie!' said Peter. 'We'll put old Scamper on guard again outside the door. And, by the way, Jack, there's no food for the meeting to have this afternoon, because we ate it all this morning, and my mother won't let me have another lot.'

'Same here,' said Jack. 'Listen, here are the others. Goodness, aren't we nice and early! It's only twenty-five past two.'

'Wuff-wuff!' said Scamper, as the usual knock came at the door of the shed, and the password was muttered by the other four members.

'Pass, friends!' called Peter, and in they all came, with Scamper at their heels. He always knew when the whole seven were there!

'Sorry, Scamper, old thing, but I want you to keep guard outside,' said Peter, and gave him a gentle push. 'Bark if Susie so much as puts her nose in at the front gate!'

Scamper put his tail down mournfully, and went to sit outside. He sensed that there was excitement about and he wanted to share it. Still Peter was the chief, and Scamper, like the others, obeyed him at once.

They were soon all sitting round on boxes and flowerpots, their eyes fixed expectantly on Peter.

'What's this sudden meeting for?' asked Colin. 'Is something up?'

'I don't know. But I thought I'd tell you and we'd discuss it,' said Peter. 'There may be absolutely nothing in it – but if there is, it's only fair that you should all share. Listen!'

They listened eagerly while Peter told them what he had seen when he had climbed up to the balcony to get Susie's aeroplane.

'As soon as we saw the plane sitting so nicely on the balcony, I shinned up a tree to get it,' said Peter. 'And when I was there I noticed that there was a red glow shining in the balcony room. There was a crack in the curtains, you see, that's how I spotted the glow.'

'But what *was* the glow? Could you see?' asked Janet, eagerly.

'Yes. It came from a gas-fire, a *lighted* gas-fire!' said Peter. 'Now, what do you make of that?'

'Somebody left it on when the house was closed, and the people went abroad,' said Barbara, promptly. 'Easy!'

'Yes. That's what *I* thought at first,' said Peter. 'But now I'm not so sure. I have a sort of feeling that I was just about to notice something else odd when Jack suddenly called me, and I was scared the gardener would come back, so I rushed away to climb down the tree.'

There was a short silence. 'But what do you mean, you were *about* to notice something,' said Colin. 'What sort of something?'

'I don't know. I've been thinking and thinking, but it's like something in a dream. You nearly remember it and it slips away,' said poor Peter, frowning hard and trying to remember what it was that had so nearly ttracted his attention. 'I *think* it was something on a table.'

'A cloth,' said Barbara, not very brightly.

'Four legs,' said Pam, with a giggle.

'Don't be silly,' said Peter, impatiently. 'It was something *unusual*, I'm sure.'

'Well, what are we going to do about this gas-fire?' said George. 'It ought to be turned off, that's certain. It's a frightful waste of gas, and there might be a danger of fire from it.'

'That's what *I* think,' said Peter. 'But how do we get it turned off?'

'Tell the gardener!' said Jack, promptly. 'Or whoever's got the keys. I suppose, Peter, there can't be anyone in the house, can there? I mean, it *is* all locked up, isn't it?'

'Yes, as far as I know,' said Peter. 'All the curtains to the windows were drawn, anyhow, and that usually means a house is locked up. I wonder who the owners are?'

'Somebody called Hall,' said Jack. 'I heard my mother say so.'

'Would your mother know who had the keys?' asked Peter. 'I mean, sometimes people give the keys to neighbours, don't they? Or to estate agents?'

'She *might* know,' said Jack. 'I'll ask her. Suppose she says the estate agents have them, we could go and tell *them* about the gas-fire then. And if it's neighbours, perhaps my mother could telephone to them and get them to go in and turn off the fire.'

'And if we *can't* find out who has the keys, we'll have to tell that old gardener,' said Janet. 'For all we know, *he* has the keys himself! Perhaps he pops into the house and lights a gas-fire to warm his toes by when he's cold!'

'Fool!' said Peter. 'Look out, that's Scamper barking. Someone's coming!'

There was a knock on the door. 'If that's you, Susie, I'll pull your hair till you yell!' shouted Jack, fiercely.

But it wasn't Susie. It was Peter's mother. 'I don't know your password!' she called, 'but I've come to say that if you'd like to ask the Secret Seven to tea, Peter, they can all stay!'

'Mother! Come in! You don't need a password if you bring news like that!' said Peter, joyfully, and flung the door wide open. 'The meeting's over. Report any news from your mother tomorrow, Jack.'

[6]

A good half-hour's work

Next morning the Secret Seven met again, very promptly. The password was muttered five times to Peter and Janet in the shed, and five times Scamper barked a welcome.

'Well,' said Peter, when the door was shut and they were all sitting in a circle in the dark little shed. 'Any news to report, Jack?'

'Not much,' said Jack. 'I asked my mother about Bartlett Lodge, and she said the owners have gone abroad for a year, and they left the keys at their bank. Mother said no one is allowed to go into the house except by permission of the bank.'

'Really?' said Peter. 'Not to clean or anything?'

'I asked her that,' said Jack. 'And she said no, not even to clean. She said that Alice, a woman who comes to do some cleaning each week, went in and cleaned it thoroughly, top to bottom, before it was locked up.'

'Ah, then what about asking Alice if she left the fire on!' said Peter, at once. 'Couldn't you ask her that, Jack? Could you talk about the house and then sort of lead round to gas-fires and electric lights and so on?'

'Well, I don't mind trying,' said Jack. 'But wait a bit, no, I can't. She's broken her arm and isn't coming for a bit.'

'Bother,' said Peter. 'Now how can we get round *that*?'

Everyone thought hard. 'Why can't you go and ask her how she is, and take her some sweets or something?' said Janet at last. 'When our old nanny is ill we always pop round with a little present.'

'All right,' said Jack, feeling that he was being asked to do rather a lot. 'Anyway, why don't you all come with me? It would be easier then. She's seen most of you.'

'Perhaps on the whole it might make things easier if we *did* all go,' said Peter, considering. 'We could tell her about the aeroplane going into the garden. That would introduce the subject, so to speak. But we wouldn't say anything about climbing up to the balcony, of course.'

'Gosh no!' said Jack, horrified. 'She might tell my mother, and I'm sure I'd get into a row if she thought we'd gone there and climbed up like that!'

'Well, what about going straightaway?' said Peter, who liked doing things at once. 'Anyone got any money to buy sweets or something? We could buy her peppermints.'

'Oh, yes, Alice likes peppermints,' said Jack. 'That's a good idea. Come on – let's go. It's a lovely sunny afternoon, and I've had enough of this shed.'

So they all went out to buy the peppermints and were given quite a lot for a pound. Off they went to the little cottage down Green Lane where Alice lived. She was very pleased indeed to see them.

'Well, there now! It's a treat to see your smiling faces!' she said. 'And you're just in time to have one of my bits of gingerbread. As sticky as can be, it is, and I know Jack likes *that*!'

The children felt that Alice was giving them as much a treat as they hoped to give her with the peppermints! She was, however, so delighted with their unexpected gift that they couldn't help feeling pleased.

'And what have you been doing, you and Susie, since I broke my arm?' she said to Jack. 'Into mischief again, I'll be bound! And have you worn your cowboy-suit yet?'

This was a wonderful opening for what they wanted to say. Jack plunged in at once. 'Oh yes, and we've flown that lovely aeroplane that Susie got. And will you believe it, it flew right over the wall into Bartlett Lodge!'

'Did it, now? That's the house belonging to the Halls,' said Alice, offering the tin of gingerbread round generously. 'I cleaned it down from top to bottom after they went. My, that was a job!'

'Did you have to draw all the curtains?' asked Peter. 'We noticed they were drawn.'

'Yes, I drew them all,' said Alice. 'The house looked so dark and dreary then that I was glad to lock it up and leave it behind me!'

'I suppose you had to turn off the electricity and water and gas?' said Janet, feeling rather clever.

'Oh, yes, I turned everything off,' said Alice. 'So if any of you are thinking of moving in there, you'll have to get me to come and turn things on again for you!'

Everyone laughed heartily at this little joke, and Peter looked triumphantly at Jack as he, too, laughed. So the gas *had* been turned off, had it? Then how did that gas-fire come to be burning there, up in the balcony room? Well, they had learnt quite a bit from Alice!

'Isn't there *anyone* there?' asked Jack.

'Nobody at all. It's all locked up now. I tell you, I locked every window and door myself,' said Alice. 'The only person who goes there is old Georgie Grim, the garden-er, and a good name he's got too! Grim by name and grim by nature. But he's honest, I'll say that for him. Have another piece of gingerbread, Jack?'

'No thanks,' said Jack. 'We must be get-ting off. I hope your arm will soon be all right, Alice. Goodbye – see you soon again, I hope!'

And with that the Secret Seven marched off, feeling that they had done quite a good half-hour's work! And now, WHAT ABOUT THAT GAS-FIRE?

[7]

An unlucky encounter

'Let's go into this field and talk,' said Peter, as soon as they left Alice's house. 'We've learnt quite a few things from her. It was a good idea to go and see her. She's awfully nice, isn't she, Jack?'

'Yes. I told you she was,' said Jack. 'But look – if she locked and—'

'Wait till we're in the field,' said Peter. 'We don't want *anyone* to overhear this. At the moment it's our own little mystery, and we'll keep it to ourselves.'

So nobody said a word till they were all sitting down in the field. Then Peter began the talk.

'It's quite clear that *Alice* didn't leave the fire on,' he said. 'And if she did as she said, and turned off water, gas, and electricity when she left, then SOMEONE has turned on at least the *gas* since she locked up the house.'

'That's right,' said George. 'But who? And what for? Surely nobody is living in the house, unknown to anyone?'

'You'd have thought old Georgie Grim would have spotted any stranger about,' said Colin, thoughtfully. 'Alice said he was honest, didn't she? Well, if he'd noticed anyone lurking about, he'd surely have reported it?'

'I think he's horrid,' said Pam. 'I bet he wouldn't bother about reporting anything!'

'Don't be silly, Pam,' said Peter. 'Just because *we* think he's horrid, because he wouldn't let us get Susie's plane, isn't any reason to think he's dishonest.'

There was a silence. Nobody could think what should be done next.

'Do you think we should tell Mother?'

said Janet at last, turning to Peter. Peter hesitated.

'I don't think she'd believe I really *did* see that gas-fire burning,' he said. 'It sounds rather unbelievable after all that Alice told us.'

'Well, we can easily prove it's true,' said Jack. 'Easily! Let's wait till that gardener goes home for the night and slip over the wall and up that tree again. We can easily peep through the curtains.'

'Yes! And if the fire *is* burning there, though we know from Alice that the gas is turned off, *then* we'll tell your mother, Peter,' said George. Everyone nodded gravely.

'Yes. It's about the only thing to do,' said Peter. 'All right. Jack and I will scout round there this evening after Georgie Grim has gone home. Jack, I'll be round at your house about half-past six. It'll still be light, and we can shin up that tree in a second.'

'Who's going to boost us up the high wall?' said Jack. 'We can't climb it without help.'

Peter considered. 'Have you a light ladder you could lug out of your shed?' he asked. 'We could easily take it into the field – it's only just behind your house! And we could go up the ladder and clamber on the wall one after the other.'

'Right,' said Jack. 'I only hope Susie isn't about. If she sees me dragging a ladder out of the shed she'll stick to me like a leech to see where I'm going with it!'

'Bother Susie!' said Peter, feeling very glad that Janet was not like the tiresome Susie. 'Well, I'll see you about half-past six, Jack. We'll have a meeting tomorrow morning at ten-thirty, down in the shed.'

'Make it eleven,' said Colin. 'I've got to go to the dentist.'

'Right. Eleven o'clock,' said Peter. 'And tonight Jack and I will have a look at the

Mysterious Gas-Fire. I bet it will be burning away merrily!'

They all went home to their dinners, feeling pleasantly excited. Jack went to his garden-shed to see if there was a ladder there. Yes. There was the old one that his father used when he pruned some of the taller fruit trees.

'Hallo! What are you doing in here?' said Susie's voice, just behind him. He jumped, and Susie laughed.

'Oho! You've gone quite red! What are you up to?' said Susie, annoyingly. 'Are you doing some job for that silly Secret Seven club of yours? Do you want a ladder by any chance?'

Susie was altogether too good at guessing! Jack picked up a little fork and a basket and marched out. He would do some weeding and show Susie she was wrong about the ladder! She followed with great interest, calling out as she went.

'Oh, what a good little boy! He's going to do some weeding! And he doesn't know the difference between seedlings and weed-lings!'

'Will you be quiet, Susie,' roared Jack, really exasperated, and pulled up a wall-flower quite by mistake.

'That's a wallflower,' said Susie at once. 'Oooh, you *will* get into trouble if you're going to pull up all the wallflowers.'

And then Jack lost his temper and pulled up two more hefty wallflower plants and shook the earth from their roots all over his aggravating sister. Susie fled, howling in dismay.

At half-past six Peter came round to the garden door at Jack's home. He saw Jack waiting for him behind some bushes. He put his finger to his mouth to warn Peter to be quiet.

'Susie's about,' he whispered, and led the way to the shed on tiptoe. He opened the door and there, sitting half-way up the ladder he so badly wanted, was Susie, pretending to read a book, grinning all over her face!

'Hallo! You don't want the ladder, do you?' she said. 'I'll get down if you do.'

Jack glared at her, and then the two boys walked out and banged the door hard. 'Now we can't even have the ladder!' said Jack, fiercely. 'I'm so sorry, Peter.'

'Don't worry,' said Peter, cheerfully. 'We'll simply not go over the wall, that's all. We'll go in at one of the front gates. It can't be helped. Come on, and do cheer up, Jack. This may be rather exciting!'

The two boys made their way out of Jack's garden and walked across the field till they came to the little lane that led to the front of Bartlett Lodge. Now they were in the road into which the drive-gates opened. They looked cautiously up and down the road.

'Not a soul in sight,' said Jack. 'I think if we walked smartly up to the first drive-gate and darted inside we'd be safe from anyone's view. Come on. If anyone appears in the road we'll simply walk past the gates, and then come back again when the coast is clear.'

They walked quickly up to the first drive-gate. Nobody appeared at all, so they darted in quickly and hid in some bushes to make sure that no one had seen them. Nobody shouted at them, so they felt sure they were safe. Keeping carefully to the bushes, they made their way round the side of the big, silent house.

'It's a gloomy place, isn't it?' said Jack, in a low voice. 'The curtains are still drawn across every window. Now, look out! We've got to sprint across this yard, so be quick.'

They sprinted across the little yard, and ran straight into two big men! One was

Georgie Grim, and the other was a big, well-dressed man, wearing a suit, and carrying a slimly rolled umbrella. They both gaped at the two surprised boys.

'Here you! What are you doing here?' said the gardener at once, and pounced on Jack before he could get away. He gripped Jack's arm so hard that the boy cried out.

'Ha! You're the boy who said his aeroplane had flown into the garden, aren't you?' said Grim, and shook Jack as if he was a rat. 'Yes, you sat up on that wall and cheeked me! Now what are you doing here? If you—'

'Let me go!' cried Jack. 'You're hurting me.'

Grim shook him again. 'Yes, and I mean to! Was it you who came into this garden and walked over the bed at the bottom of that old tree? Was it you who climbed up the tree to the balcony? Oh, I saw the footmarks below, and I saw the marks where you'd climbed the tree! That I did! What were you doing up there, I'd like to know?'

'Our aeroplane landed on that balcony, that's all!' said Peter. 'We climbed the tree to get it. We couldn't help treading on the bed below, but there weren't any plants in it, only weeds!'

'Now look here, my lad,' said the other man in a pleasant, well-spoken voice, 'it's a serious thing to come trespassing into a private place, you know. And if this is the second time, as Grim here says, I'm afraid you're going to get into trouble. What are your names and addresses?'

Peter's heart sank. Gosh, now his father would hear about this and be angry, and Jack would get into trouble too.

'Honestly, sir, we weren't going to do any harm,' he said.

'Either you tell me honestly what you are doing here this evening, or I shall get Grim to go for the police – with you, boy, still in his grip,' said the stranger, sternly. 'I'm not the kind of person that lets bad boys get away with anything. If you tell me the truth, though, I may think twice about the police.'

'Well,' said Peter, desperately, 'I *will* tell you! Our aeroplane flew over the wall, and landed up there on that balcony. And Jack and I came to get it. I climbed up the tree to the balcony, and just as I was going to get down again, I had a look round at the balcony room, and I saw something odd.'

Both Grim and the stranger looked at him sharply. 'And what was the odd thing you saw?' asked the second man.

'The curtains up there don't quite meet,' said Peter. 'And when I peeped between them I saw a gas-fire burning in the room. I really did!'

'And we came back tonight to climb up again and see if it was still burning,' said Jack, still in Grim's steely grip. 'And if it was we were going to tell our parents, and they would ring up the police and—'

Grim gave a sharp exclamation. 'What! You saw a gas-fire burning? Impossible!' He turned to the other man. 'You're from the bank, aren't you? You've come to see if everything is all right? Well, it *is*, and what's more all the gas is turned off at the main, so this boy is telling lies! You can't have a gas-fire burning without gas!'

'I tell you I DID see it,' said Peter. 'And I was jolly astonished.'

'Well, this is a most amazing story,' said the man in the suit. 'I'm Mr Frampton, from the bank, and I came here to pay Grim his wages this evening and to see if everything was all right. You seem decent lads, not the little hooligans I thought you were at first. But really, if there's no gas it's difficult to believe your tale.'

'Have you got the keys with you?' asked Peter, eagerly. 'Couldn't you unlock the place, see if the gas really *is* turned off, and go up to that balcony room where I saw the fire? Just in case.'

'Hm, well, it seems rather a waste of time,' said Mr Frampton, putting his hands into his coat-pocket, and bringing out a Yale key labelled Bartlett Lodge No 2. 'But I think on the whole that I'd better go into this. Let that boy go, Grim. I'm inclined to believe they are not after any mischief. Now, where is the front-door key? Ah, here it is. We'll go in and see if there's any truth in this extraordinary tale!'

In a short while they were all in the big hall of Bartlett Lodge. Grim, looking as dour as his name, marched Mr Frampton to the kitchen, and showed him the gas-meter, the electricity switch, and the tap to the water main.

'Every one turned off, as you can see,' he said. Mr Frampton looked at them, and nodded.

'Right. Now let's go upstairs to this balcony room where the mysterious gas-fire is supposed to be burning. Lead the way, Grim, lead the way!'

[8]

Peter is very angry

Grim led the way, first up one wide flight of steps and on to a fine long corridor, and then up another flight of stairs to the second floor. The house seemed very dark because of the drawn curtains, and Mr Frampton stumbled once or twice. It smelt musty and shut up, too.

'Here's the balcony room,' said Grim, opening a door. A crack of light came in through the place where the curtains did not quite meet. Grim went across and drew them apart with a noise that made everyone jump.

Peter looked for the gas-fire. Yes, there it was, but no red light glowed from it! It stood there, unlit and cold! He stared at it in silence, unable to believe his eyes, for he had felt certain that it would be just as red and glowing as it had been when he had peeped in from the balcony and seen it.

Mr Frampton made a clicking noise of exasperation. 'Well! You've been making up a nice little story, haven't you, my boy? This fire is certainly not alight and can't have been before either, because all the gas is turned off. You should know better than to make up tales like that. I'm ashamed of you. You seem quite a decent lad, too. Well, Grim, shall we hand them over to the police and let them tell their fairy-tale to *them*, and see what the police have to say about it?'

Grim shook his head. 'I reckon the police have enough to do these days, without having to listen to silly tales like this. The boy made the whole thing up to amuse all his friends, and then made the tale an excuse to come trespassing.'

'I did *not*!' said Peter, angrily. 'And I'd like to tell you—'

'That's enough!' said Mr Frampton, sharply. 'And now, just listen to me. I will NOT have you children trespassing like this, whether it's to fetch balls or aeroplanes or anything. And I'm not listening to any more excuses or tales. If Grim had wanted to hand you over to the police I would have done so with pleasure, but he's let you off, and so will I – just this once! Grim, if you have any more trouble with these boys, ring me up and I'll deal with them.'

'Right,' said Grim, sounding extremely pleased.

'But I've got something else to—' began Peter, desperately, but Mr Frampton snapped at him at once.

'Silence! I will not listen to another word. I thought you were a decent lad. I'm mistaken, it seems. Get down the stairs and out of the gates before I chase you out with my umbrella.'

Peter gave Mr Frampton such a glare that Jack was quite astonished. Whatever was the matter with Peter? He had been proved wrong, so why did he go on arguing and interrupting? He took Peter's arm and pushed him to the stairway.

'Come on, idiot,' he said. 'Let's go while the going's good. You made a mistake. It's no use arguing about it!'

Looking very angry indeed, Peter went down the stairs with Jack, and out of the front door. He slammed it hard, and the noise echoed all around. It made Jack jump in fright, and he stared at Peter, really astonished.

'What *is* the matter?' he said. 'Surely you're not in a rage because you were proved wrong, Peter, old chap?'

Peter didn't answer. He took Jack's arm and led him at top speed down the drive and into the road. He didn't say a word all the way down the little lane to the field, and not until they were well out in the middle of the field did he open his mouth to the puzzled and rather scared Jack.

Then he turned and faced him. 'So *you* think I was mistaken too, do you?' he said. 'Well, I'm *not*. That fire was alight when I saw it. I don't care tuppence if the gas and the electricity and the water and everything else is turned off – *that fire was alight*. SOMEBODY had turned it on and lit it. SOMEBODY had been in that room – and done other things, besides lighting the gas, too!'

Jack stared at Peter, amazed. '*What* other things?' he said. 'And why didn't you tell Mr Frampton?'

'I *tried* to. You know I did!' cried Peter. 'And everytime I tried he snapped at me and shut me up! I shan't tell him anything! I'll solve the mystery myself!'

'Wait a minute, Peter. Tell me. What other things did the person do besides lighting the gas-fire?' asked Jack, wondering if Peter had gone slightly mad.

'Listen. Do you remember I said that I had *almost* noticed something in that room, besides the gas-fire, yesterday morning?' demanded Peter. 'And I couldn't call to mind what it was because just as I was noticing it, you shouted at me?'

'Yes. I remember,' said Jack. 'What was it, then?'

'Well, I noticed a plant in a pot,' said Peter. 'A plant my mother grows in her greenhouse, called a primula. The flowers are rather like big polyanthus. And I noticed that the plant was alive and healthy, not all dead and withered as it *should* have been, left in an empty house for weeks. Primulas need a lot of water.'

'You mean someone had been watering it?' asked Jack.

'Yes,' said Peter, beginning to calm down. 'I looked into the pot just now and the soil was wet. Someone had watered it not later than yesterday. AND I noticed something else, which *you* should have noticed too if you'd been a *good* member of the Secret Seven!'

'What?' asked Jack, surprised again.

'I noticed that the clock on the mantel-piece was going,' said Peter. 'And it's only an eight-day clock. So *someone* must have wound it up during the last week, mustn't they? And I thought the room smelt of tobacco smoke too. Oh, somebody has been living in that room, I'm pretty sure!'

'Gosh!' said Jack, astounded. 'But who, Peter? And why?'

'That's for the Secret Seven to find out,' said Peter. 'Go round to everyone and re-mind them that there's an important, MOST IMPORTANT meeting at eleven o'clock sharp

tomorrow morning. And don't let that tiresome Susie know a *thing* about it! This is
very, very secret!'

[9]

Peter gives his orders

Again the Secret Seven were extremely punctual, and the password, 'Lollipops', was said briskly as all the members arrived at the meeting-shed, greeted excitedly by Scamper.

'What's up, Peter?' said George, seeing Peter's rather grim expression as he sat waiting in the shed for everyone. 'You look sort of boiling up inside.'

'Well, I am,' said Peter, relaxing into a short grin, and then looking grim again. Clearly something big was happening, and the Secret Seven settled down expectantly, feeling little thrills as they looked at their chief. Whatever was he going to tell them?

Very shortly and clearly Peter told them of his and Jack's visit to Bartlett Lodge, and how they had been caught by Grim the gardener and Mr Frampton from the bank, the man who held the keys of the locked house.

Then he told them how he had persuaded Mr Frampton to go into the house and find out whether the gas really was turned off or not (and what a sigh all the members gave when he had to confess that it *was* turned off after all); and then went on to describe how they had gone up to the balcony room, and seen the fire unlit (another disappointed sigh!) and then, and then . . .

The next part was truly exciting, of course, especially when he told about the ticking clock. The members gazed at Peter in real admiration. Here was a chief indeed! Why, he had behaved like a first-class detective, and he had stood up to Grim and the man from the bank like a hero!

'You should have *seen* Peter when he came out of that house!' Jack said, when Peter had finished his tale. 'He was in such a rage that he slammed the front door till it nearly fell off its hinges! And his face was as red as fire, and . . .'

'That's enough,' said Peter, his face looking almost as red as fire once again, he was so embarrassed at Jack's praises. 'Anyone would have felt as I did. Honestly, I kept *on* trying to tell Mr Frampton about the clock, and the plant, and the smell of smoke, but he simply wouldn't listen.'

'What a stupid man!' said Barbara. 'To think he could have noticed all those things and didn't. Still, *Jack* didn't notice any of them either, did he?'

'That's enough, Barbara,' said Peter again, seeing *Jack's* face go red now! 'We've got a most peculiar mystery on our hands, and we've got to get to the bottom of it ourselves. This is something that the Secret

Seven really *can* rack their brains over. Now, how can we find out who's been in the house, and if he was still there, hidden somewhere while Grim and Mr Frampton went in and out, and if Grim knows anything about it? And if anyone *is* hiding there, what's his reason?'

'We'd better try and find out if Grim really *has* got a name for honesty,' said George. 'If he has, and everyone speaks well of him, we'll know it's nothing to do with *him.*'

'Yes. That's a good point,' said Peter. 'Does anyone know somebody who has employed Grim at any time?'

'Yes. My granny did for a year,' said Pam. 'I didn't like him at all then, because he wouldn't let me pick even an unripe gooseberry when I went to tea with Granny!'

'Hm! That sounds rather honest than otherwise!' said Colin.

'Or mean!' said George. 'Hadn't Pam better go and ask her granny a few questions, Peter?'

'Yes. That's a job for you to do today, Pam,' said Peter, looking at her. 'I want a report this afternoon about that.'

'Right,' said Pam, feeling important, and writing it down in her notebook, though she knew she couldn't possibly forget.

'We really ought to find out where Grim lives and see if we can discover if he's at home each night,' said Peter. 'It might *possibly* be Grim making himself nice and comfortable at Bartlett Lodge. I mean, he might have a horrid wife who nags him, say, and he goes and sleeps in that house just to get away from her, now he's got the chance. I bet he knows how to get into the house, even though he hasn't got the keys.'

'I think that's a bit far-fetched,' objected Barbara. 'About his nagging wife, I mean.'

'We can't leave anything to chance,' said Peter, firmly. 'Nothing is too far-fetched to examine. Grim is an important person in this mystery. The more we know about him, the better.'

'All right,' said Barbara, hastily. 'But all I hope is that I don't have to go and interview a nagging wife!'

'Well, you *will*,' said Peter, to Barbara's horror. 'You and Janet can go together, once we've found out where he lives. Pam's granny will be able to tell her that, I expect.'

'Do we have to find out if Mr *Frampton* is all right?' asked Jack, beginning to feel that there was going to be a lot of snooping round in this mystery!

'Yes. I can ask my father that,' said Peter. 'I expect he'll know him, or know *of* him. But I don't somehow think Mr Frampton *really* comes into this.'

'What else do we do?' asked George.

'Well, when we've found out all we can about Grim, and have made up our minds about him, I shall probably decide to set a watch on Bartlett Lodge,' said Peter, in a most business-like tone. 'There's a good shed there, within view of the kitchen-door, which, I imagine, would be the likeliest place for any mysterious person to enter or leave the house. One or other of us must be on watch all the time. I am quite DETER-MINED to track down the person who lives secretly in that balcony room.'

'It's terribly exciting,' said Pam, feeling quite breathless with all this sudden plan-ning. 'I think you're a very good chief, Peter. I do really.'

'So do I,' said Jack, and the others agreed.

'Well, we'll soon see if I am or not,' said Peter, getting up. 'Time will tell! Oh, by the way, there's a new password for next time, as we've had our last one for a long time.'

'What is it?' asked Jack.

'Grim!' said Peter, smiling. 'Just that. Grim! And don't you forget it, anyone!'

[10]

The girls do very well

Pam felt very important as she went off to see her granny immediately after her midday dinner. She had her notebook in her pocket, and a freshly sharpened pencil. I may have to write down all kinds of details for Peter, she thought. What fun it is to belong to the Secret Seven. We just NEVER know what kind of job we'll have to do next.

Her granny was in her back garden, snipping off dead daffodils. She was very pleased to see Pam.

'Why, Pamela!' she said. 'I didn't expect you this afternoon. Have you come to have tea with me, dear?'

'No, I'm afraid not, Granny,' said Pam.

'I've got orders from Peter to interview you about someone.'

'Good gracious!' said Granny, surprised. '*Interview me*? What about?'

'About a gardener you once had, called Georgie Grim,' said Pam, taking out her notebook. 'You see, Granny, the Secret Seven is on to a mystery again, and we're interested in Grim because we think he's got something to do with the mystery.'

'You and your mysteries!' said Granny, laughing. 'You really amuse me. Well, well, if it's Peter's orders, you must do as you're told. Now, what do you want to know?'

'Was Grim honest, Granny, when he was with you?' asked Pam.

'Absolutely,' said Granny, and Pam wrote that down, wondering if she was spelling it right. 'Abslootly honest,' she wrote.

'Er – did he ever have to look after the house when you went away?' asked Pam.

'Yes. During the year that he worked for me, he and his wife came and lived in the house for a month, while we were away,' said Granny. 'And the wife kept the place spotlessly clean. She was a thin, pale woman, with a cough, I remember.'

'Wait a bit, you're going too quickly,' said Pam, writing down all this at top speed. 'How do you spell "spotlessly"? Oh, it's all right – I know.'

'Any more questions?' said Granny, amused. 'I feel as if you were a policeman questioning me, Pamela!'

Pam laughed. She was quite enjoying this, and couldn't help feeling that she was doing it very well. She bit the end of her pencil and wondered what to ask next.

'Er – did you miss anything from the house when you came back?' she said.

'Not a thing!' said Granny. 'And what was more, Mrs Grim had made a lot of jam for us, and bottled a great deal of fruit, and wouldn't take a penny for it, because she said she had enjoyed staying in the house so much. I must say the little woman looked a good deal better for the month she spent here. Dear me, am I going too fast for you, darling? Let *me* write it all down for you.'

'Oh, *no*,' said Pam at once. 'This is *my* job, Granny. Just say it all again slowly, and I'll soon get it down. Are there two Ts in "bottle", do you suppose?'

'There are usually,' said Granny. 'Well, well, I must say that I admire you Secret Seven. You certainly go into things thoroughly. *Do* stay to tea.'

'I wish I could, but Peter wants this information this afternoon,' said Pam. 'Well, thanks awfully, Granny. You've given me some surprising news. We all suspected Grim might be doing something he'd no right to do.'

'And what was that?' said Granny, quite overcome with curiosity.

'Oh, it's a secret,' said Pam. 'We're never supposed to talk about our mysteries while we're solving them. Goodbye, Granny, and thank you very much.'

She skipped off happily, her notebook safely in her pocket. Pam was not often entrusted with important things by Peter, and she felt rather proud of the way she had written down Granny's answers to her questions. In fact, she thought herself quite clever!

Peter and the three boys were in the shed with Scamper when Pam arrived. 'Lollipops!' she said, as she knocked at the door. There was no answer.

'Let me in!' called Pam. 'I said the password.'

'You didn't, whoever you are,' called Peter's voice.

'I'm Pam, and you *know* it's me!' said Pam indignantly. 'I've got a lot of news. Let me.'

'Password, please,' said Peter.

'But I've already s—' began Pam, and then she suddenly remembered the *new* password. 'Oh, sorry, Peter – Grim, Grim, GRIM!'

'Once is quite enough,' said Peter, and opened the door. 'Well, did you see your granny?'

'Yes,' said Pam, and beamed round happily. 'Here are my notes, with my questions and Granny's answers. I wrote everything down.'

Peter took the notes and read them out aloud, much to Pam's delight. He shut the little notebook and nodded at Pam.

'Very good, Pam. A very nice piece of work. Well, it seems as if Grim is honest enough, and his wife too. In fact the wife sounds really nice. It's rather surprising, really, because I couldn't help feeling that bad-tempered old Grim was the one who had broken into Bartlett Lodge somehow.

it seems as if somebody *else* must be ...e, someone that Grim knows nothing about, for if he did he would certainly report it, as your granny says he's absolutely honest.'

'It's funny, isn't it?' said George. 'Well, we'll certainly have to find out who it is.'

'Yes, we must keep a watch on the kitchen-door, as I said,' decided Peter. 'Hallo, here comes Janet and Barbara. They've been to find out about Mrs Grim. I wonder if they'll remember the new password!'

A knock came at the door. 'Grim,' said Janet's voice, and then came a giggle. '*Mr Grim.*'

'And *Mrs* Grim!' said Barbara. Peter opened the door, grinning.

'Come in, idiots,' he said, 'and tell us your news!'

The two girls came in and sat down. Scamper gave them an enormous welcome.

'Hallo, Pam!' said Janet. 'What did your granny say about Grim?'

'Oh, she says he's absolutely honest,' said Pam. 'Here are my notes about it. I wrote them down.'

Janet and Barbara were impressed with the notes. 'You didn't spell the word "absolutely" the right way,' pointed out Barbara. 'Oh, Peter, *we* didn't make notes. We only just asked questions and remembered the answers.'

'That's all right,' said Peter. 'Janet, what happened? Make your report, please.'

'Well, we went down to where Grim lives,' said Janet. 'I found out from the postman; it was quite easy. Oh, Peter, it's a *dreadful* little cottage. Really dreadful.'

'Why? What's it like?' asked Peter.

'It's near the canal, and built so low that it's on a level with the water,' said Janet. 'And you know we've had a lot of rain this year, so the canal water has risen quite a bit, and it has overflowed into the little cottage garden . . .'

'And the ground floor of the cottage must be TERRIBLY damp,' said Barbara. 'And do you know, we even saw fungus growing all the way up one wall! It's really horrible.'

'It's in very bad repair too,' said Janet. 'Daddy would never let *his* cottages get like that, Peter. Our farm-men's cottages are palaces compared with Grim's. I can't think how he stands it. There's quite a big hole in the roof, where some tiles have fallen off.'

'No wonder they were so happy when they looked after my granny's house one summer,' said Pam. 'And no wonder Granny said Mrs Grim looked thin and ill. Anyone would, if they lived in that damp, smelly cottage down by the canal!'

'I wonder they don't move,' said Jack.

'Well, it's hard to get a cottage these

days,' said George, 'especially at a low rent. Did you find out anything about Mrs Grim, Janet? Did you see her?'

'No, we didn't,' said Janet, 'but we talked to the woman next door. Her cottage is built much higher than the Grims', and it's quite dry. She saw us looking round the Grims' place, and called out to know what we wanted.'

'And we just said we were looking at the quaint old cottage!' said Barbara. 'Which was perfectly true, of course. And we asked her who lived there, though *we* knew it was Grim's cottage.'

'You did well,' said Peter, approvingly. 'Go on. What did the woman tell you?'

'Well, she told us what we already knew – that Grim has a daily job, keeping that big garden going at Bartlett Lodge, and that he comes home about six o'clock each night. And that his wife isn't well, so he does all the shopping in his dinner-hour, and cooks a meal at night. And she said that Mrs Grim was a nice little woman . . .'

'And she's very fond of Grim,' said Barbara, anxious not to be left out. 'Gosh! Fancy anyone being fond of surly old *Grim.*'

'Mrs Grim must be quite ill,' said Janet. 'Her neighbour says she hasn't been out to hang her washing up for a whole week. Grim even does that, too!'

'Well, *I* think he sounds rather a nice old boy, even though he's so bad-tempered with us,' said Peter, rather astonished at all this news. 'Pam's granny says he's quite *honest*, and if he does all that for his wife, he must be kind as well.'

'I expect it's living in that dreadful damp cottage that makes him surly,' said Barbara, who really had been shocked to think of anyone living in such a horrid little hole. 'Peter, you wouldn't even let one of your *pigs* live in a place like that.'

'I should think not!' said Peter. '*Our* pigs have wonderful sties, and they're cleaned out twice a day.'

It suddenly began to dawn on everyone that their reports had not helped the mystery in the least. In fact, what they had learnt actually wiped Grim right out of the picture, and left them with nobody to suspect at all, except perhaps Mr Frampton, the man from the bank. But Peter had something to say about him.

'*He's* all right. My father's known him for years,' said Peter. 'I just mentioned casually that I'd met him, and Dad said, "Oh, Frampton, he's a fine chap, quite a friend of mine. Where did you meet him?"'

'Gosh, what did you say to *that*?' asked Jack, remembering their meeting with the man, and how nearly they had got into serious trouble. 'How did you answer?'

'Well, Scamper barked at that very moment, and I just didn't answer the question, but asked Scamper one instead!' said Peter, with a laugh. 'I said, "Who's coming, Scamper, who's coming, old boy? Let's go and see who you're barking at!" And out of the room we went.'

There was another silence. A cold, flat feeling slowly came over the Seven. Where did they go from here? Was there anything they could do to solve the mystery now, except what Peter had suggested before – watch the kitchen-door of Bartlett Lodge from the little shed opposite it? But they *knew* it wasn't Grim going into the house. Would they ever see any intruder at all? They couldn't watch the doors and windows! It would have been easy enough just to watch the kitchen-door when they felt sure it was Grim going in and out; but suppose the intruder, whoever he was, never came and went at all, but simply stayed hidden in the house, turning on the gas at the main whenever he wanted a little warmth, or to boil a kettle!

'Let's talk and plan,' said Peter, at last. 'Now, has anyone a good idea, a really good one?'

No one said a word at first, and then Jack spoke up. 'Well, Peter, the only thing *I* can think of is for one of us to climb that tree up to the balcony tonight, and watch for a light to come on in that room, and peep through the crack in the curtains to see who it is. That's my idea!'

[11]

An astonishing discovery

The rest of the Seven stared at Jack in admiration. 'Why ever didn't we think of that before?' said Peter. 'Of course whoever is hiding there would feel quite safe at night, with Grim gone home, and nobody about at all. We might see something really interesting if we watch up on the balcony!'

'Bags I go,' said George, at once.

'*Four* of us will go,' said Peter. 'One of us must be on guard at the gate to warn the others if someone comes in there. We don't want to be caught. One of us must also be at the bottom of the tree to warn the ones on the balcony if anyone comes. I think Jack and I will climb the tree and be the balcony watchers – we've been up there before.'

'Can I come too?' said Janet, longingly. 'It's beginning to sound awfully adventurous!'

'No you can't come,' said Peter, 'or there will be too many. The four of us will go together when it's really dark.'

'Let's ask if we can go to the cinema,' said Jack. 'And not stay till the end, but slip out about eight o'clock and go to Bartlett Lodge.'

'Good idea,' said Peter. 'Right, we'll all meet at the cinema. You others can come too, if you're allowed, but you'll have to sit right through the programme, if your parents will let you stay as late as that.'

'Mine won't,' said Barbara, sadly. 'At least I don't think so. Oh, I shan't be able to sleep tonight for wondering what's happening to you four boys.'

A very pleasant feeling of excitement warmed the hearts of the Secret Seven for the rest of that day. Even Scamper felt it,

and was most bitterly disappointed when
Janet and Peter went off to the cinema
without him after tea.

He sat down sadly in a corner. Now he
would have a long, long wait till he could
bark and jump and wag his tail again!

None of the Secret Seven paid that much
attention to the picture at the cinema, and
yet it was a good one, all about a wild pony,
the kind they usually loved. The four fid-
geted and looked at their watches, wishing
the time would go quickly, so that they
might leave, and go about their night adventure!

At ten to eight Peter whispered to Jack.
'We'll go! I can't sit still a moment longer!
Tell the others.'

Peter led the way. It was dark outside
now, and they needed their torches. It was a
cloudy night and not even a star showed in
the sky.

They made their way to Jack's house and

slipped in at the back gate. 'Watch out for Susie!' said Jack, in a low tone. 'She's in tonight.'

But there was no sign of the aggravating Susie, much to Peter's relief. They went across the field at the back of Jack's house and down the little lane into the road beyond, where Bartlett Lodge stood.

'Now,' said Peter, halting. 'You know your orders, all of you. Colin, watch by the gate. Hoot like an owl if anyone comes in. George, you're to stand at the foot of the tree that we're going to climb to the balcony. You're to hoot too, if you see or hear anything suspicious. Jack, have you got your torch ready? We'll need it to climb the tree.'

Jack put his torch between his teeth, and so did Peter, as soon as they began to climb the tree that grew up to the second-floor balcony. This meant that they could use both their hands for climbing, and yet could see where they were going, though rather awkwardly.

Colin was at his post by the gate, hiding behind a bush. George was at the foot of the tree, listening intently for any unusual sound. He could hear Jack and Peter cautiously climbing the tree. Then he could hear the slight scrape of their rubber shoes as they climbed over the stone balcony. Now a great disappointment for Peter and Jack – no longer could they see through the crack in the curtains! Someone had pulled them carefully together, so that not the tiniest chink remained for them to peep through! The boys were bitterly disappointed!

'Look at that! We can't possibly see into the room now,' whispered Jack.

'Yes, but it shows someone has been into the room again!' said Peter. 'It may even mean that somebody is there *now*.'

They pressed their noses against the closed window, trying in vain to see inside.

They saw nothing, but they suddenly heard sounds, sounds which surely came from the inside of that little room!

'Listen!' whispered Jack. 'What is it?'

'It's a radio being played very, very quietly,' said Peter. 'We can hardly hear it. I'm sure that's what it is. Would you believe it! Who in the world is in there?'

They had now switched off their torches, and were in complete darkness. They stood there, wondering what to do. How did the intruder get into the house? Mr Frampton appeared to be the only one with the keys of the house; not even Grim had one. And anyway they had proved that he was absolutely honest. Then had some outsider a key? Or did he perhaps get in through a coal-hole? Or was there an unfastened window somewhere? All these things went through the boys' minds very quickly, and then something happened that made them jump violently.

An owl's hoot sounded from the front of the house! It must be Colin giving the arranged warning. The two boys stiffened at once. And then, to their horror, another hoot came, this time so near to them that they jumped in fright again. It came from the bottom of the tree.

'Danger!' said Peter. 'Keep quite still, Jack. Something's going to happen!'

The two boys on the balcony stood absolutely still, and hardly breathed. And then they heard a sound that made them stiffen again in fright.

'Someone's climbing up the tree!' whispered Peter to Jack. 'I can hear him – and see the light of his torch!'

'What can we do?' said Jack, trembling. 'He will see us here. We can't hide anywhere on this balcony.'

'No. But we can quickly scramble up the tree a bit higher and hide in the leaves,' said Peter, pulling Jack to the tree. He could now

hear the climber's heavy breathing farther
down the tree. Thank goodness he was slow
at climbing!

'Quiet now!' whispered Peter, as he and
Jack climbed back into the tree and further
upwards. They then stayed quite still, peering through the leaves down at the balcony
below.

A man was climbing up the tree to the
balcony, his torch in his mouth. As he came,
a warning owl-hoot sounded again from
below. The man was now climbing over
the little stone pillars of the balcony, and
stood below the boys, taking his torch from
his mouth. Jack and Peter in the tree above
could see the light shining brightly.

The man went to the window and
knocked. It was a special knock – three
long ones, two short ones and then two
long ones. Knock-knock-knock. Knock-
knock. Knock-knock.

The boys held their breath and peered

through the leaves cautiously. They saw the curtains drawn back from the window, and immediately a light streamed out from the room inside. Then someone unfastened the window and opened it.

As the light streamed out on to the balcony, Jack and Peter saw the man who stood there, saw him quite clearly and recognised him! They could hardly believe their eyes!

The man went swiftly through the window, shut it behind him and drew the curtains across so that not a chink of light showed. Only when the window was shut did the two boys dare to breathe. Then Peter clutched Jack.

'Did you see who it was, Jack?'

'Yes. *Surely* it was old Grim the gardener!' said Jack, quite astounded. 'What did *you* think?'

'Yes – it *was* Grim! But who would have thought it! *Grim*! The honest Grim! No wonder he was angry when he discovered our footmarks at the bottom of this tree, and saw that *we* had climbed it too, and had used his own private way into the house!'

'But who's *in* there?' said Jack, feeling bewildered. 'It must be the someone who lit the gas-fire and wound up the clock, and watered that plant! Is it some burglar there busy packing up things for Grim to take away?'

'Goodness knows!' said Peter, as puzzled as Jack. 'I suppose it was Grim who had carefully turned off the gas at the main last night when we all went in to see the house. He must have seen our footmarks under the tree by then and have been afraid we might have seen the gas-fire and tell tales about it. So he quietly turned off the gas at the main, in case anyone said they'd seen the fire, because it's plain there couldn't be a fire without gas. I was jolly puzzled about that, weren't you?' 'Very,' said Jack. 'Well, what do we do now? Better climb down, I think, because I'm sure we can't see anything more here at the moment. We'd better find Colin and George – they'll be worried about us.'

So they climbed carefully down the tree again, making no noise at all, nor daring even to switch on their torches. They felt carefully with their feet before they made a step downwards, and were soon at the bottom.

There was no sign of George. 'He may think we are the man who climbed up,' whispered Jack. 'What about saying our password, Peter? He'll know it's us, then.'

'I was just going to,' said Peter. 'Grim!' he said, in a piercing whisper. 'Grim!'

'Here I am!' said George, from a nearby bush. 'Gosh, I was glad to hear the password! I was afraid it might be that man again! Did you hear my hoot?'

'Yes. And Colin's too,' said Peter. 'Let's

go and find him. This mystery has got very mysterious, all of a sudden!'

They found Colin hidden by the front gate, and gave him the password. He appeared as soon as he heard it. They all slipped out of the gate and down the road, and were soon in the little lane leading to the field behind Jack's house.

They stopped in the middle of the field, having been completely silent since leaving the front gate.

'Who was that man? Did you see?' said Colin at once.

'It was Grim!' said Peter. 'Would you believe it! Grim, the man we had ruled out completely. What *can* he be doing there?'

'Pretty mean of him to leave his sick wife all alone each night in that horrible cottage,' said Colin. 'He must have a pal in Bartlett Lodge and be planning to rob the house in peace and quiet while the owners are away.

There's nothing to stop them taking things bit by bit.'

'Shall we tell the police?' asked George.

'I don't know. I rather think I'll tell my father,' said Peter. 'You see, he knows Mr Frampton, the man who has the keys of the place. We'd better leave it to them as to what to do. Gosh, who'd have thought it was Grim after all!'

'Well, I never liked him,' said Colin. 'Horrid, bad-tempered man. Come on, let's get on. I'm beginning to feel as if there may be quite a lot of Georgie Grims in this dark field, waiting to pounce on us. Hurry up!'

'We'll go to my house and tell my father straightaway,' said Peter. 'You must all come with me. There'll be a lot to tell, and you'll have to back me up. Let's go by the cinema and see if the others are out. They really ought to be in on this.'

They went down the road that led to the

cinema, and saw the people streaming out –
and the three girls with them! Peter ran up.

'Hey, you three! You're to come with us.
Something very strange has turned up, and
we're all going to my house to tell my
father. *He'll* know what to do!'

[12]

Peter's father takes over

The four boys told the excited girls what
had happened. When they came to the part
where Jack and Peter had actually heard
someone climbing up to the very balcony on
which they were standing, Pam gave a loud
squeal.

'Oh! I should have been scared stiff! Oh,
who was it? I'm jolly glad I wasn't there!'

'It was old Georgie Grim!' said Peter.
'What do you think of *that*? And to think
we'd quite decided that he was honest and
kind and all the rest of it! Anyway, it's a
serious matter now. That's why we're going
back to tell my father.'

Peter's father and mother were most
astonished to see everybody coming in

together. 'Why Colin – Jack – Pam, Barbara, George – whatever are you doing
back here instead of going home?' said
Peter's mother.

'Mother, we've got something to tell
you,' said Peter. 'Dad, you'll be surprised
when you hear it! You see, the Secret Seven
have—'

'Don't tell me you've tumbled into another adventure!' said his father. 'You haven't got yourselves into trouble, have you?'

'Oh, no,' said Peter. 'And – well, I hope
you won't be cross when you hear the
things we've done.'

'Begin at the beginning,' said his mother,
taking down a tin of biscuits and handing
them round. 'You're the chief of the Seven,
aren't you, Peter? Well, you begin, then.'

So Peter began the strange story, right
from the morning when Susie's aeroplane
had flown over the wall into the garden of
Bartlett Lodge, and disappeared. He told of

the angry gardener, of how he and Jack had discovered the aeroplane on the balcony and climbed up to get it . . .

'And it was *then* that the mystery really began,' said Jack, interrupting. 'Wasn't it, Peter? Because when Peter peeped in between the drawn curtains of the balcony windows he saw a gas-fire merrily burning away there!'

How astonished Peter's parents were to hear the story and to listen to the way the Seven had proved Grim's honesty, and his kindness to his wife, and then, to cap everything, they heard the astonishing ending!

'There we were, up in the tree six foot above the balcony, trying to see who it was coming knocking on the window of that curtained room, and when the curtains were pulled and the light streamed out we saw who it was.'

'And who *was* it?' said Peter's father, really excited.

'It was *Grim*,' said Peter. 'Yes, it really was, Dad! Someone from inside opened the window, and he got in, and the curtains were drawn across and the window fastened!'

'And we thought we'd better come and tell you because you know Mr Frampton, who has the keys,' said Jack. 'We felt sure you would know the best thing to do.'

'That was sensible of you,' said Peter's father. 'Well, I'm blessed! The things you Seven get up to! And yet I can't find fault with you for anything you've done in this matter. You were very sensible and most courageous, and now, of course, we must at once go after this fellow Grim, and see what he's up to. Thanks to you, we shall catch him in his lair with his burglarious friend, whoever he is!'

'His burglarious friend!' said Pam. 'That sounds exciting. What are you going to do, please?'

'I'm going to ring up Mr Frampton, get him to come round with the keys of Bartlett Lodge, and he and I will go together to surprise Grim and his friend in their cosy lair,' said Peter's father, getting up to go to the telephone.

'Dad! Dad, can we go too?' cried Peter, afraid that at this most exciting moment he was going to be left out.

'I'll see what Mr Frampton says,' said his father, and dialled his number. The children listened to the one-sided conversation in silence, their hearts beating fast. What an adventure this had suddenly turned into! Oh, if only they were allowed to see the end of it!

Peter's father rang off and turned to the waiting children. 'Mr Frampton is extremely interested, as you can imagine. He's coming round straight away and will pick me up here in his car. He says Peter and Jack may come too, as they will be able to state again that they actually saw the gas-fire burning the day before yesterday. They'll be what we call witnesses.'

'Can't we others come?' said Janet, dolefully. 'Oh, I do want to, Dad.'

'I dare say you do,' said her father. 'But you must realise that we can't have the whole Seven of you trailing after us in what may be quite a serious matter. Mr Frampton is going to ring up the police, and ask them to stand by in case he telephones from Bartlett Lodge for help. We shall have to find out first if it really *is* a police matter – and it probably is.'

Jack and Peter felt a great big surge of excitement welling up inside them. They grinned at one another in joy. They were going to be in at the end. What would happen? What would Grim say? And who was his 'burglarious friend'?

In a few minutes there came the sound of a car hooting at the front gate. Peter, his father, and Jack hurried out, followed by the envious gazes of the others. Then Janet's mother set to work to ring up the other children's parents and tell them not to worry; the Secret Seven were at her house!

Jack and Peter got into Mr Frampton's car, and sat silently in the back. They still remembered how angry he had been with them only a short time ago! He said nothing to them, but spoke briefly to Peter's father, and then drove off to Bartlett Lodge.

Jack squeezed Peter's arm in excitement. 'We're bang in the middle of a real adventure!' he said, in a low voice. 'Whatever do you suppose is going to happen next?'

[13]

Inside the empty house

The car drew up outside Bartlett Lodge. The house looked absolutely dark, not a light to be seen anywhere. They all got out, and Mr Frampton spoke quietly as they stood beside the car.

'I propose that I unlock the front door, and that we all go in silently,' he said. 'It is imperative that we make no noise at all, for we don't want to give any warning to those fellows inside. We will go straight up to the same room that these boys took me up to before and surprise the men there, and demand an explanation. Now, follow me.'

They followed him in at the drive-gate, and up to the front door. He cautiously slid the key in, turned it, put a second key into a lock below, and turned that also. The door opened with a small creak.

Mr Frampton walked in quietly. The others followed, and he shut the door silently. He switched on his torch and spoke in a whisper.

'The telephone is here, in that corner. You, boy – what's your name, now?'

'Peter,' said Peter.

'Well, you, Peter, will have to be the one to nip down to the phone and call the police if we have any trouble,' said Mr Frampton. 'Just say that I want someone sent along here at once. Is that clear?'

'Yes,' said Peter, and again felt the uprush of breathless excitement that all adventures bring.

'Now, quiet,' said Mr Frampton, and led the way upstairs, his torch shining steadily in front of him. The stairs were well carpeted, and their footsteps made no noise at all. The men went first, the two boys followed. Jack was so excited that he felt quite breathless.

Up the first flight of stairs, on to the wide landing, and then very, very quietly up the second flight. Again there was a landing, but not such a wide one. Mr Frampton stood quite still at the top, and then switched off his torch.

A line of light showed under one door, the door of the balcony room! From inside came a murmur of voices and then suddenly the voices became raised, and the four outside could hear shouts and threats!

What was going on in that closed room? Jack felt himself shaking at the knees. 'It's all right,' whispered Mr Frampton, feeling Jack trembling against him. 'They've got the radio on, they're listening to a play. Don't be scared!'

Jack was most relieved. Only the radio! Of course! He and Peter had heard it before,

when they had stood outside on the
balcony! Mr Frampton now strode forward
to the closed door and turned the handle,
but he turned it in vain! The door was
locked on the inside!

Mr Frampton raised his hand and
knocked most imperiously on the door,
shouting at the same time, 'Open this door
at once!'

The radio in the room was switched off
suddenly and now there was nothing but
silence. Mr Frampton knocked again. 'I said
OPEN THIS DOOR!'

'Who's there?' said a voice from inside.

'Open the door, and you'll soon see,'
roared Mr Frampton, making both boys
jump violently. 'I know your voice, Grim!
The game's up. Open the door, or it will be
the worse for you and your friend!'

There was a silence for a few seconds,
and then Grim's voice came again, sounding most upset. 'It's you Mr Frampton, isn't

it? You haven't got the police with you, have you? You know I'm an honest man, you—'

'I've no police here at the moment,' thundered Mr Frampton, 'but I'm sending someone down to telephone them in one minute's time, if you do not open this door! As for your honesty, I fear it will be difficult for you to prove that, Grim.'

There sounded a hurried few words from inside the room, as if Grim were reassuring someone. Then he spoke again, in a most beseeching voice.

'Mr Frampton, I'll open the door and come out to you, if you'll let me shut it after me and will not come into the room till I've spoken to you.'

'You'll open this door, and we shall come in straightaway,' said Mr Frampton, angrily. 'What nonsense is this? And I warn you, Grim, that if you let your friend get away through that window it will be the worse for you. Have done with this nonsense, man, and OPEN – THIS – DOOR!'

The door still did not open. Mr Frampton turned to Peter and spoke to him in a loud voice, so that Grim could hear it inside the room.

'Peter, go down into the hall and ring up the police as I told you. Tell them to send someone here immediately.'

'Right,' said Peter, but before he could take more than two steps there came a cry from Grim.

'No! Don't get the police! I'll open the door. Wait, wait!'

'Wait, Peter,' said Mr Frampton, in a low voice. 'I think he's come to heel.'

Nobody moved. They heard a key turning in the lock on the other side of the door, the handle turned, and the door opened. Grim stood there, his surly face lined and worried.

'Once more, I beg of you, don't come into

this room,' he said, holding the door so that no one could see into the room. 'I do beg of you.'

'Stand aside, man,' said Mr Frampton, and pushed him sternly to one side. He stepped into the room, followed by Peter's father. The two boys came last, wondering whatever they were going to see.

Nobody in the least expected to see what was there! They stood silent, staring in astonishment.

[14]

A great surprise

The little balcony room looked clean and cosy. The gas-fire burned steadily, and the clock on the mantelpiece ticked merrily. The table was set with a small white cloth, and on it was a loaf of bread on a wooden platter, a dish of butter, and a plate of yellow cheese.

But these were not the things that surprised the four visitors. Their eyes were fixed on one corner of the room, where there was a couch near the fire. On it lay a woman, a little old woman with white hair and white face, whose hands trembled as her scared eyes watched the four come into the room.

Mr Frampton stopped abruptly in astonishment. He, like the others, had expected to see another man, some 'burglarious friend'. But there was no one to see except the frightened old woman.

'Please,' she said, in a trembling voice. 'Please, it's all my fault. Don't be hard on Georgie.'

Mr Frampton spoke in a surprisingly kind voice. 'Now don't get upset, old lady. We've only come to see what's happening here.'

Tears suddenly rolled down the old woman's cheeks. Grim went over to her and took her hand. 'Now, now,' he said, 'don't you fret. I did it for the best.'

Then he turned to Mr Frampton. 'You see, it was like this. My wife, she's not strong, and her cough has been bad all winter. The doctor said I'd have to take her away from that cottage of ours, too damp he said it was, and he said he'd get her into a hospital . . .'

'And I wouldn't go,' said the old woman. 'I can't be separated from Georgie. I'd die, I know I would.'

'And then the canal water rose with all the rain we had, and the water came into the house,' said Grim, in a desperate voice. 'And some tiles came off and the rain came through into our bedroom. Well, what was a man to do? I couldn't find another place to go to, and here was this big house, all empty, and we only need one small room, and I was at work here . . .'

'I see,' said Mr Frampton, sitting down on a chair. 'Yes, I see. So you managed to get your wife here, into a warm, dry room, and you turned on the gas and the electric light and the water . . .'

'Yes. I got in through the coal-hole the first time, and went up into the kitchen, and unlocked the door,' said Grim. 'You had taken the key, but I knew where a spare one hung on a hook on the dresser. And I brought my old wife here one night, and a terrible walk it was for her . . .'

'And you made her comfortable here, Grim?' said Mr Frampton. 'And did the shopping, and the washing, and hung it out behind your old cottage? Yes, I know all about that, you see! And then you climbed in each night through the balcony window.'

'Yes,' said Grim, dolefully. 'And I was in a rare temper with these boys here, when I knew they'd been up that tree outside, and on to the balcony, and what a fright I had when they told you about seeing the little gas-fire here. I tell you, I've been in a real state all the time. Yes, I know I did wrong, but what was a man to do?'

'You could have come and asked me, Grim,' said Mr Frampton.

'And you'd have said no!' cried Grim. 'Look here, and you too,' he said, turning to Peter's father. 'My old woman, she's done what she could in the house while she's been here. She's dusted every day, ill as she is, and she's watered every plant, and she's polished every bit of furniture. She was scared to death all the time, but I will say this, her cough's better.'

Peter suddenly found that there were tears in his eyes. Poor Grim! And his poor, ill old wife, in that dreadful damp cottage with a hole in the roof. After all, they had done no harm. In fact, Mrs Grim had dusted and polished and watered, and done as much as she could!

There was a little silence. Then Mr Frampton spoke in a gentle voice. 'Well, Grim, I shall have to report this to the owners, of course, but I shall point out your difficulties, and say that Mrs Grim has kept the house dusted and polished, and . . .'

'You won't get the police, will you?' pleaded the little old woman, from her couch. 'My Georgie, he's a good man, honest as the day, and kindness itself. He's got a temper that gets him into trouble now and again, but he's a good honest man, and *I* ought to know!'

'I shan't get the police,' said Mr Frampton. 'But as you know, perhaps, the owners are coming back next week. You will not be able to stay here then.'

'I'll go back to my old cottage then,' said Mrs Grim. 'My cough's better since I've been here, this warm, dry place. I'll be all right now in our cottage.'

'You won't!' said Grim, suddenly sounding desperate again. 'They'll put you somewhere away from me. They'll say you're ill, and they'll take you away!'

'Now, listen, stay here until I hear from the owners,' said Mr Frampton. 'I can see you are to be trusted. But if you're in trouble another time, ask for help from some friend, Grim. Don't do things like this.'

'I'd have done that, but I thought my wife might be taken away from me,' said Grim. 'I'm sorry for the trouble I've caused, but we've done no harm, that I can promise you.'

Peter's father stood up. 'Come along, Frampton,' he said. 'Let's leave them in peace. Grim, come along to me tomorrow and I'll see that you are supplied with milk and eggs for your wife. Good night, Mrs Grim. Cheer up. We'll see what can be done for you and Grim. Good night, Grim.'

'Good night,' said Grim, and the two men, followed by the two boys, went out of the room, leaving Grim standing at the door, worried and anxious.

'Dad!' said Peter, looking as anxious as the old gardener. 'Dad, can't we do *some-thing*? I shan't be happy till we do!'

Three cheers for the Secret Seven!

The next morning there was another Secret Seven meeting in the old shed. One after another the knocks came, and the password.

'Grim!'

'Grim! It's me, Pam.'

'Grim! Can I come in?'

Peter opened the door five times, and Scamper barked five times too. Soon everyone was there. They all looked rather nervous, for the events of the night before had surprised and shocked them.

'To think that we hated Grim so much, and all the time he was worried in case we found out his poor, precious secret!' said Janet.

'I *can't* bear to think of them having to go back to that awful cottage,' said Barbara. 'Old Mrs Grim will get a dreadful cough again. But they'll have to turn out of Bartlett Lodge in a few days. Oh dear, this mystery is having a rather horrid end.'

'We've GOT to do something to help them,' said Jack. He pulled a purse out of his pocket, and emptied some money on to the top of a wooden box. 'Look, I've emptied my money-box and Susie's too, and I've brought all the money along in case it will be any use.'

'*Susie's* money-box!' said Janet, amazed. 'But did she say you could?'

'Yes. I told her all about last night when I got home,' said Jack. 'After all, you know, it *was* her aeroplane that started this adventure. Wasn't it?'

'Yes,' said everyone, nodding.

'So I thought Susie ought to hear the

story,' said Jack. 'And she told me to take *all* her money, too.'

'Gosh! People are most surprising!' said Barbara. 'Good old Susie!'

'Well, now,' said Peter, 'does everyone want to give money to help the Grims? And is there anything else we can do? I dare say our money would help to mend that hole in the cottage roof. We've got to do *some-*thing! I shan't feel happy till we've tried to make up for spying on old Grim, and bring-ing his precious secret to light.'

Everyone most willingly agreed to help. Peter felt proud of his Secret Seven. There wasn't a mean, ungenerous person among them! Jolly good!

Scamper suddenly began to bark, and a knock came at the door.

'Password!' shouted Peter.

'I don't know it,' said his father's voice.

'Oh, it's you, Dad! We'll let you in with-out the password!' said Peter, and opened the door. His father came in, and smiled round at everyone. He saw the money on the top of the box and raised his eyebrows.

'My word, somebody's rich!'

'Oh, that's money to help old Grim and his wife,' said Peter. 'Jack brought it, half is from Susie too. We're all going to bring some, Dad. We're so sorry for thinking those awful things about Grim, and for spying on him, when all he was doing was taking care of his wife.'

'Yes. It was a very sad story, wasn't it?' said his father. 'I felt as upset as you did, Peter. I'm glad you want to help. So do I!'

'How can *you* help, Dad?' said Peter, astonished.

'I'll tell you,' said his father. 'You know that little cottage that our old cowman has just left? Well, I'm going to have it done up straightaway, and offer it to old Grim. We need a man to trim the hedges and so on, and if he likes to come to our farm here and work, he can have the cottage and live there with his wife. It's sunny and dry, and she'll be all right there.'

'Dad! Oh Dad! I do love you!' cried Janet, and almost knocked her father over with a great bear-hug. 'We couldn't *bear* to let the Grims go back to that dreadful old place of theirs. Oh, how wonderful to be a grown-up and do things like that!'

'And how wonderful to be young and to belong to the Secret Seven!' said her father. 'You're a set of meddling youngsters, you know, but somehow your heads and hearts are sound, and you do the right thing in the end! Well, I'm glad you found out Grim's secret. Now we can set his mind at rest, and our own too.'

'And we'll give you all our money to help to pay for putting the cowman's old cottage right,' said Jack. 'We meant to help somehow with the money, and we will!'

'Thank you,' said Peter's father. 'Give it

to Peter, and he can give it to me. And let me
say this, all of you. You've had many adventures before, you Secret Seven, but I
don't think you'll ever have one that has
such a satisfactory ending. And one more
thing – I'm very, very proud of you all!'

He stood up, smiled round at everyone's
pleased face, and went out. Peter looked
round, his face glowing.

'Did you hear that, Secret Seven?' he said.
'Did you hear that, Scamper? Three cheers
for the Secret Seven! Hip-hip-hip . . .'

'HURRAH!' shouted everyone, and Scamper barked madly. What a curious adventure it had been – and all because of Susie
and her aeroplane!